MW00964204

10-14

AUG 2 5 2005

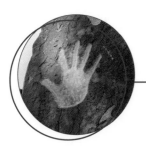

CULTURE
in Australia

Melanie Guile

Chicago, Illinois

For information, address the publisher:
Raintree, 100 N. LaSalle, Suite 1200, Chicago, IL 60602

Customer Service: 888-363-4266
Visit our website at www.raintreelibrary.com.

Printed in China by WKT Company Ltd.

09 08 07 06 05
10 9 8 7 6 5 4 3 2 1

Library of Congress Cataloging-in-Publication Data

Guile, Melanie.
  Culture in Australia / Melanie Guile.
       p. cm. -- (Culture in--)
  Includes bibliographical references and index.
  ISBN 1-4109-1132-2 (hc, library binding)
  1. Australia--Civilization--Juvenile literature. I. Title II. Series: Guile, Melanie. Culture in-- .

  DU107.G85 2005
  306'.0994--dc22

                                2004016648

Acknowledgments
The publisher would like to thank the following for permission to reproduce photographs: AAP Image/AFP: p. 23 (upper), /AFP Photo/William West: p. 18, /Damir Ivka: p. 17; AFP Photo: p. 24; Art Gallery of New South Wales/Lin Onus, Wiradjuri, Melbourne, Fruit Bats, 1991, polychromed fibreglass sculptures, polychromed wooden disks, Hills Hoist clothesline, 250 x 250 x 250 cm overall, © Lin Onus, Licensed to VISCOPY, Sydney, 2003, photograph: Jenni Carter for AGNSW (acc#395.1993.a-c): p. 27; Art Gallery of South Australia, with permission from Aboriginal Artists Agency Ltd: p. 26; Coo-ee Picture Library: pp. 6, 7, 10, 11, 12 (both), 16, 25; Corbis/Reuters/Mark Baker: p. 9 (lower); Grundy Television Pty Ltd: p. 23 (lower); Harper Collins Australia/© Janet Glad 1918: p. 21; National Gallery of Victoria: p. 28; Newspix: p. 19, /Pip Blackwood: p. 9 (upper); Nolan Gallery, Cultural Facilities Corporation, Canberra: p. 29; Penguin Books/Peter Mack: p. 20; Skyscans/David Hancock: pp. 13, 14, 15.

Cover photograph of Rugby World Cup 2003 Opening Ceremony reproduced with permission of APL/Corbis/Photo & Co./Manuel Blondeau.

Every effort has been made to contact copyright holders of any material reproduced in this book. Any omissions will be rectified in subsequent printings if notice is given to the publishers.

The paper used to print this book comes from sustainable resources.

Disclaimer
Some of the images used in *Culture in Australia* may have associations with deceased indigenous Australians. Please be aware that these images may cause sadness or distress in Aboriginal or Torres Strait Islander communities.

CONTENTS

Some words are shown in bold, **like this.** You can find out what they mean by looking in the glossary.

CULTURE IN *Australia*

The vast continent of Australia is the flattest and driest land on Earth. The northern part lies in the tropics and the southernmost island, Tasmania, is in the freezing Southern Ocean, which surrounds Antarctica. Australia is a land of huge distances. The city of Perth in Western Australia and Darwin in the Northern Territory are closer to Asia than they are to the country's eastern states. The **indigenous** people of the continent are called Aborigines. In addition, Torres Strait Islanders are people that live on the islands off the northern coast. They have lived in the country for more than 40,000 years and have a rich culture.

European settlement of Australia began when Great Britain established a **penal colony** in New South Wales. It was claimed for Great Britain by the English explorer Captain James Cook in 1770. The first fleet of prisoners arrived in Port Jackson in Sydney under Captain Arthur Phillip in 1788. They struggled to survive in a hostile land, suffering from starvation and sickness, as well as from the brutal treatment by the British guards. The prisoners' experiences helped mold the Australian values of friendship, equality, making do with little, grim humor in difficult times, and disregard for authority.

Great Britain stopped sending prisoners to Australia's eastern states in 1853, soon after gold was discovered there. As the country grew wealthy and free settlers flocked in, the people demanded **independence** from Great Britain. In 1901, the Australian colonies formed one self-governing nation, the **Commonwealth** of Australia, with the English **monarch** as its head of state. This is still the case, although many are now calling for Australia to break its last ties with Great Britain and become a **republic.**

What Is Culture?

Culture is a people's way of living. It is the way in which people identify themselves as a group, separate and different from any other. Culture includes a group's spoken and written language, social customs, and habits, as well as its traditions of art, crafts, dance, drama, music, literature, and religion.

A Capital Idea

Sydney, Australia's largest city, is home to four million people. It is not, however, the capital. In 1901, when the Australian colonies combined to create one nation, rival cities Sydney and Melbourne fought over which should be the capital. So, a new city, Canberra, was built roughly halfway between the two cities.

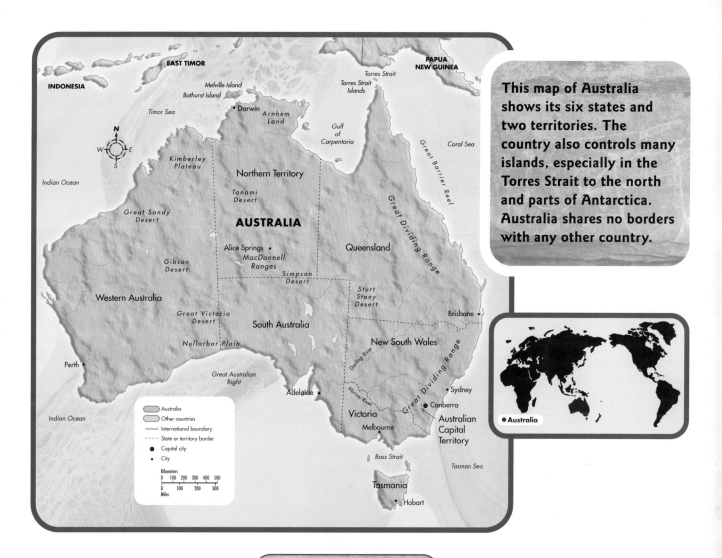

This map of Australia shows its six states and two territories. The country also controls many islands, especially in the Torres Strait to the north and parts of Antarctica. Australia shares no borders with any other country.

Flag of Australia

Australia's flag has the British flag in the upper left corner. It represents Australia's ties to Great Britain. The large "Commonwealth Star" under the British flag represents Australia's states and territories. The five smaller stars are the Southern Cross, a **constellation** visible from all over Australia.

For many years, the Europeans that had settled Australia borrowed their culture from Great Britain, which until the 1950s they often referred to as "home." Australians considered themselves rough and practical. Culture was something that happened overseas, and the creative life of indigenous peoples was also ignored. This "cultural cringe," as it became known, is now largely gone. Today, Australians are proud of Aussie—as people from Australia are sometimes called—talent throughout the world. Indigenous cultures are also celebrated. The casual, outdoor lifestyle blends comfortably with a sophisticated arts scene, cutting-edge performances, a vibrant literary community, and some of the world's finest restaurants. The stunning opening ceremony at the 2000 Olympics in Sydney sparked many Aussies into a renewed pride in their culture.

The People

Australia is a large country with a population of twenty million people, about 85 percent of whom live in the coastal cities. Sydney and Melbourne are the largest cities, but Canberra, with fewer than half a million people, is the nation's capital. Indigenous people make up about 2.4 percent of the population. **Fertility** is low at 1.8 children per woman, and the number of elderly people is growing rapidly. Australia's population would be in decline without the 100,000 immigrants who arrive each year.

Since World War II (1939–1945), immigrants have enriched Australia's culture. **Mosques** and temples now stand alongside **Christian** churches. Some of the country's best-loved performers and writers come from immigrant backgrounds. Asian and European cuisines, or cooking styles, make eating out a world-class experience. Australia is now a **multicultural** society, and **ethnic** traditions and languages are officially recognized.

People from many different cultures enjoy Australian life at this Melbourne restaurant.

The Lucky Country

Australia is often called the Lucky Country because it is a safe place, and Australians have a relaxed outlook on life. Wages are high by world standards. Education is free and **compulsory** to age sixteen, and just about everyone can read and write. Forty-two percent of the population goes on to higher education. There is low-cost national health care and pensions for the elderly and unemployed. Life expectancy is high, at just over 80 years. The government is chosen in **democratic** elections, and voting is compulsory.

Environment in Danger

Since European settlement, Australia has had one of the world's worst animal **extinction** rates. Today, about 1,400 species are **endangered**—the second-highest number of threatened species in the world. Australia also has the fifth-highest rate of **land clearance** in the world. The Great Barrier Reef in northeastern Australia is under threat from shore pollution. Australians are the world's highest per head producers of **greenhouse gases,** yet the country has not signed the Kyoto Protocol, an international agreement that is designed to reduce **global warming.**

Nevertheless, about half a million people in Australia are unemployed, and pensions barely meet people's needs. Australia has a history of racism. Aboriginal and Torres Strait Islander peoples have always suffered **discrimination** and are very disadvantaged compared with other Australians. Today, immigrants who arrive by boat and seek **asylum** in Australia are often imprisoned or turned away. **Sexism** is also a problem. Few women hold top jobs, and there has never been a female prime minister. Although Australians generally consider themselves to be **egalitarian,** there is a wide and growing gap between rich and poor.

Underdog Heroes

Australia's greatest heroes are underdogs who struggled bravely against the odds. Ned Kelly (1854–1880) is a national hero, even though he was a **bushranger** who was hanged for murdering three police officers. He gained the people's sympathy by speaking out against police **corruption** and injustice. And Australia's most celebrated battle was actually a defeat, not a victory. During World War I (1914–1918), the Australian and New Zealand Army Corps (ANZAC) landed at Gallipoli, a beach in Turkey, to attack the enemy. But they were sent to the wrong place and found themselves facing sheer cliffs with the enemy at the top. Despite this, they fought for eight months before retreating.

Ned Kelly, one of Australia's most famous underdog heroes, has inspired songs, books, and movies.

CUSTOMS
and Celebrations

Australians are known for their casual and laid-back manner. "No worries, **mate**" and "Not a problem" are common sayings. They tend to disregard class or **status** and generally favor the underdog. In fact, an attitude called the tall poppy syndrome means that high achievers are often disliked or joked about—except if they are sports stars. Honesty and straight talking are valued, and excessive politeness is viewed with suspicion.

Humor

Dry, understated humor is used a lot, especially among friends. A typical way to show admiration for someone is to jokingly tease them. Outright flattery is very rare. A love of quirky humor has produced famous comic performers such as Barry Humphries (Edna Everage) and Paul Hogan (Crocodile Dundee).

Special Events

The Tamworth Country Music Festival is a huge annual gathering. Singer-songwriter Slim Dusty (1927–2003) is Australia's best-known country singer, and many would recognize his song, "Rain Tumbles Down In July."

The Laura Dance and Cultural Festival is an **indigenous** arts festival held every second June in an ancient bora ring—a kind of dancing place—in Cape York, in far north Queensland. It showcases Aboriginal and Torres Strait Islander arts, crafts, dances, and songs.

Todd River Regatta

Alice Springs in the Northern Territory is home to one of the world's quirkiest events, the Todd River **Regatta.** This boat race is unusual because the river in which it is held contains no water. In wacky, homemade bottomless boats, teams race along the dry creek bed and end the day with a huge water-cannon fight.

The Adelaide Festival of Arts, held every second March, was Australia's first arts festival and specializes in opera, theater, and some modern works. The huge Festival of Sydney held each January features international acts and outdoor concerts. Melbourne is the live venue center of Australia, and its comedy festival held each March and April is one of the world's biggest.

Anzac Day

Anzac Day is April 25 and commemorates the ANZAC soldiers who fought bravely against the Turks at Gallipoli in 1915 during World War I (1914–1918). Dawn prayer services are held at war memorials, and a **bugler** plays "The Last Post" as the sun rises. Military parades are held, and diggers, or veterans, gather to remember their fallen mates.

Celebrations

Christmas is the biggest festival of the year in Australia. People buy presents for their friends and families and decorate their houses. Families gather for a meal, sometimes of traditional turkey and plum pudding, but often have barbecues outside in the summer weather. Australia is in the Southern Hemisphere, and the seasons are reversed there. July is the middle of winter, and December is the middle of summer. For New Year's Eve, people gather for celebrations and fireworks displays. New Year's Eve also marks the beginning of the long summer holidays.

Ethnic groups celebrate their own festivals. Greek communities hold street processions and church services on Easter and share traditional colored eggs. During the Vietnamese Moon Lantern Festival in September, city streets come alive with night lantern parades. In central Victoria, Bendigo's famous Chinese dragon—the world's longest—dances at the Easter Festival.

ETHNIC GROUPS

Australia is one of the world's most **ethnically diverse** countries. About 25 percent of the people were born overseas, some 200 languages are spoken, and about 100,000 new immigrants arrive each year from 170 countries. But it was not always this way.

The First Immigrants

The first immigrants to Australia were prisoners, mostly from England and Ireland. This **Anglo-Celtic ethnic group** formed the dominant culture from 1788 to 1850. The discovery of gold in 1851 led to 50,000 newcomers arriving every year, many of them Chinese. Through hard work, they were often very successful in finding gold. Other gold miners resented this, and riots led to the first **immigration restrictions** on nonwhites.

The White Australia Policy

The 1901 Immigration Restriction Act introduced the infamous dictation test. Nonwhites wanting to enter Australia first had to pass a written test in any European language chosen by the testers. Almost everyone failed. The law was popular in Australia, however, where fear of large Asian populations to the north led to widespread racism. The White Australia Policy was gradually ended after World War II (1939–1945), when labor shortages led the government to encourage immigration from some non-European countries. The dictation test was abolished in 1958. In 1973, the government under Prime Minister Gough Whitlam finally removed race from the immigrant selection process.

This Vietnamese grocery store shows how many ethnic groups have set up small businesses, transforming Australia's cities.

Greek Australians perform a traditional dance at a cultural festival.

Multiculturalism

The idea of **multiculturalism** arose in 1972 with the head of immigration Al Grassby. He encouraged the preservation of ethnic languages, cultures, and traditions, along with loyalty to Australian values. Since then the idea has won widespread acceptance. The government funds a host of ethnic activities, including arts festivals and support services. Today, Australia is regarded as a **tolerant** society, where many ethnic groups live and mix together.

New Australians

New Zealanders make up the largest immigrant group in Australia. The wave of immigration following World War II (1939–1945) brought large numbers of Italians, Greeks, Dutch, Maltese, Yugoslavs, Turks, and Lebanese. These "new Australians" traveled cheaply under the government's Assisted Passage program during the 1950s and 1960s. Many settled in low-cost, inner-city neighborhoods; set up businesses; and succeeded. Since 1975, many Vietnamese, South Africans, Chinese, and Indonesians have arrived. These ethnic groups swelled the country's population from seven million in 1945 to twenty million in 2004. They transformed Australia from an English-Irish outpost into a vibrant, complex culture.

Boat People

When the **Communists** won the Vietnam War (1965–1975) in 1975, many Vietnamese who had supported the losing side fled the country. Some risked sailing in leaky boats to Australia. These refugees became known as boat people. In contrast to today's immigration policies, under which asylum seekers are imprisoned on arrival, the boat people were accepted and given help to settle in the country. Today, about 160,000 Vietnamese make up the third-largest ethnic group in the country.

11

INDIGENOUS
Culture

Australia's **indigenous** peoples are the Aborigines who live on the mainland and the island of Tasmania, and Torres Strait Islanders who live on the northern tropical islands. In all, they number about 450,000 and make up about 2.4 percent of the population. One-third live in cities, while the majority remain in remote desert communities.

There are hundreds of different clans or groups with their own languages, customs, and traditions. About 60 percent of indigenous Australians identify with a specific group, and 21 percent speak an indigenous language. Each group has a strong spiritual bond to its country, where its guardian spirit, or protector, lives. Communities in the **outback** run farms and **ecotourism** businesses or work in partnership with mining companies. Indigenous Australians also live and work in the main cities. The Aboriginal and Torres Strait Islander Commission (ATSIC) oversees indigenous affairs. However, indigenous Australians, like everyone else, are ruled by the state and national governments.

Aboriginal people have their own flag, which was designed by Harold Thomas in 1971. It was first flown in Canberra at the Aboriginal tent embassy set up in front of the house of Parliament. The tent embassy was a demonstration to get the government to grant **land rights** to indigenous peoples. The Torres Strait Islander flag was designed by Bernard Namok of Thursday Island and adopted in 1992.

Aboriginal and Torres Strait Islander Flags

In the center of the Aboriginal flag is a yellow disc that represents the sun. The black field stands for indigenous peoples, and the red field represents Earth.

The green color in the Torres Strait Islander flag stands for the land, the black for the islander people, and the blue for the sea. The white shape is a traditional headdress (*dari*), and the five-pointed star represents the five main island groups.

Although relations between indigenous and other Australians are now generally peaceful, many Aboriginal and Torres Strait Islander peoples feel they have been treated unjustly. A movement for **reconciliation** calls for understanding and cooperation among all Australians and acknowledgment of the wrong done to indigenous peoples.

The Dreamtime

The spiritual world is called the Dreamtime in indigenous culture. Ancient Dreamtime stories explain how the spirits created the land, animals, plants, and human beings. One story tells how a great Rainbow Serpent slithered across the land forming gorges, rivers, and mountains as it went. Each clan has its own rituals, duties, and beliefs—its dreaming—that are performed at **sacred sites.** Traditionally, indigenous Australians had no written language, so stories and rituals were handed down by word of mouth. Songs, chants, dances, and sacred artwork were used in these rituals.

Totems

Each indigenous person has a totem, which is a spirit animal or plant linked to the dreaming. This totem is usually chosen by the pregnant mother based on a sign she receives. For example, she might have a dream about a wallaby, a small kangaroo, in which case her child's totem would be the wallaby. Each person has a special link with his or her totem animal or plant.

These men from the Ramingining community wear turtle totems painted on their backs while taking part in a cultural festival.

Bush Medicine

Traditionally, older men and women were the healers. They used rituals and bush medicine to cure their patients. Small balls of earth were swallowed for stomach pain, and mud, ash, or cobwebs were applied as bandages. Herbal medicines included gum leaves crushed or smoked over a fire so the patient could **inhale** them, and ointment was made by crushing leaves with animal fat. Many traditional **remedies** are now widely used, including eucalyptus oil for colds and tea tree oil as an antiseptic.

Health Issues Today

Europeans brought new diseases such as measles and smallpox, which wiped out entire clans. European foods also had a negative effect on the local people. The health of indigenous people is still not as good as that of other Australians. Their life expectancy is twenty years lower, and they have high rates of heart disease and diabetes. Aboriginal health services are working to improve this situation.

A health worker attends to a young patient at an Aboriginal health clinic in the Northern Territory.

The Stolen Generation

From 1910 to 1970, between 20 and 30 percent of indigenous children were stolen from their parents and put into institutions or white foster homes. It was government policy that indigenous children were to be raised in the same way as white children in order to stamp out their indigenous ways. This policy had a terrible effect on indigenous communities. Stolen children lost their sense of belonging and were often abused. In 1995, the government set up the Inquiry into Separation of Aboriginal and Torres Strait Islander Children from their Families, which found that the policy was both racist and wrong.

An Aboriginal teacher in the Northern Territory instructs children in the Yolngu language.

Pioneers of Aboriginal Rights

Neville Bonner (1922–1999) had only one year of schooling but rose to become the first Aboriginal person to be elected to Parliament. Inspired by the 1967 **referendum** that gave indigenous people citizens' rights, Bonner went into politics. From 1971 to 1983, he campaigned tirelessly for his people. He was awarded the **Order of Australia** in 1984.

Eddie Mabo of the Meriam people of Torres Strait went to the Australian High Court to fight for the right of indigenous peoples to own their traditional lands. In June 1992, the court agreed that Australia was not "empty land," as the Europeans claimed when they first arrived. The Mabo judgment opened opportunities for indigenous **land-rights** claims.

Values

In indigenous culture, sharing and cooperation are very important. People live in large family groups, and everyone takes care of the children. Many communities run their own schools and teach in both English and indigenous languages. Children generally prefer to learn by watching others and practicing. The children reach very high standards with those methods.

Sports Stars

Many indigenous Australians have achieved greatness in sports, particularly in Australian rules football, track and field, and boxing. Stars include sprinter Cathy Freeman, two-time Wimbledon tennis champion Evonne Goolagong Cawley, and Olympic-winning hockey player and runner Nova Peris-Kneebone. Lionel Rose won the world bantamweight boxing championship in 1968. Current greats include Gavin Wanganeen and Andrew McLeod in Australian rules football and Wendell Sailor in rugby.

PERFORMING ARTS

 A wide range of performing arts flourishes in Australia. Classical music and dance are state-funded, traditional and modern theater thrives, and Australian ballet and opera have gained international reputations. Arts festivals in all the major cities encourage new and original works, and rock, folk, blues, jazz, and pop music are alive and well.

Traditional Aboriginal Music and Dance

For thousands of years, Aboriginal people have gathered for celebrations that involve dancing, singing, and music. Both men and women sing during initiation or coming-of-age ceremonies and to bring rain, tell stories, or mourn the dead. Traditional dances often involve foot stomping and slow arm and body gestures to imitate animals such as the emu, frog, or brolga—a dancing bird.

Aboriginal Instruments

Aboriginal instruments include handheld hollow clapping sticks, shell or seedpod rattles, and boomerangs that are knocked together. The most famous instrument is the didgeridoo, which is made from a long hollow branch. The player blurts into it with pursed lips to create a deep, rhythmic droning sound.

Many indigenous people keep alive aspects of their ancient culture.

Indigenous Music Today

Indigenous musicians have created distinctive new styles. Jimmy Little was Australia's first Aboriginal pop star and is still making hits after 40 years. Known for his quiet manner and velvet voice, Little has been named an Australian Living National Treasure for his contributions to Australian culture and heritage. Archie Roach is one of Australia's best-known Aboriginal performers. This singer-songwriter, born in 1956, was taken from his family and raised by white foster parents. His debut single "Took the Children Away" (1990) expresses the pain of being one of the stolen generation. The song won a Human Rights Achievement Award.

The band *Yothu Yindi* is led by the highly respected Mandawuy Yunupingu. The band includes non-Aboriginal people and uses Western instruments as well as the didgeridoo.

Multitalented Star

Torres Strait Islander Christine Anu is best known as a pop singer-songwriter for her 1995 award-winning **debut** CD, *Stylin' Up*. But Anu also has other talents. She is a professional dancer, theater performer, and film actor, landing a role in Baz Luhrmann's *Moulin Rouge!* and starring in several musical theater productions.

Yothu Yindi is Australia's most famous indigenous band. Their music combines Western rock with songs, dances, and instruments of the Yolngu culture of the Northern Territory. Yothu Yindi's debut album, *Homeland Movement* (1989), was a huge success. Mandawuy Yunupingu is the band's lead singer and guitarist. He is respected throughout Australia as a thoughtful and courageous worker for his people. In 1992, he was named Australian of the Year.

Bangarra Dance Theater

Established by Carole Johnson in 1989, Bangarra Dance Theater marked a new direction in modern Australian dance. Under the creative guidance of its long-term artistic director, Stephen Page, Bangarra blends traditional Aboriginal and Torres Strait Islander cultures with modern dance styles. Performances feature athletic movements, powerful stories, and stunning set designs. Bangarra played a key role in the 2000 Sydney Olympics opening ceremony with its work *Awakenings*.

Classical and Modern Dance

The Australian Ballet is famous for its fresh, lively performances. Legendary Russian star Rudolph Nureyev danced with the company in the film version of *Don Quixote* (1973), which is considered the finest ballet film ever made. The company's most famous dancer was Robert Helpmann (1909–1986), who helped make classical ballet popular in Australia.

Dein Perry took the world by a storm with his hugely successful show, *Tap Dogs*. It features tough-looking workers in steel-tipped boots pounding the stage with great energy. The construction themes come from Perry's background in the steel mills of Newcastle, north of Sydney.

Dancers from the Australian Ballet perform a modern interpretation of *Swan Lake* in Sydney in 2002.

Theater

Dozens of theaters showcase local writing and performing talent. David Williamson is the country's best-known play and script writer. He focuses on the way people react to crises. Many of his works, including *Don's Party* (1971) and *Brilliant Lies* (1993), have been made into films. Hannie Rayson's characters struggle with truth and personal relationships. Her play *Hotel Sorrento* was made into a successful film in 1994. The Bell Shakespeare Company, run by actor-director John Bell, gives a modern slant to the great English playwright William Shakespeare's (1564–1616) plays.

Opera Divas

Australian Nellie Melba (1861–1931) was the world's most famous opera singer for almost 40 years. She delighted audiences with her clear, high voice but was also renowned for her larger-than-life personality. She gave so many farewell concerts that she inspired an Australian saying, "More farewells than Nellie Melba!" Joan Sutherland (1926–) was moved to sing after hearing Melba's records. Her 1959 London performance in Donizetti's *Lucia di Lammermoor* made her an instant star. Known as La Stupenda, Sutherland was named the greatest voice of the the 1900s. A current star is **soprano** Yvonne Kenny, who is well known in England and Europe for her many fine recordings.

The Australian rock band, INXS, is known all over Europe and North America.

Rock and Pop Scene

INXS is Australia's most successful rock band. Their lead singer, Michael Hutchence, gained world fame as a solo artist before his death in 1997. Hard rock band AC/DC also won international acclaim, as did Cold Chisel, whose singer Jimmy Barnes later achieved solo success.

Local pop legend John Farnham, also known as the Voice, had his first hit in 1967. His 1986 album *Whispering Jack* held the record for highest sales until 2003, when singer-songwriter Delta Goodrem overtook it with her soft-pop album, *Innocent Eyes*. Nick Cave's gravely voice and moody, original songs have a wide cult following. Rock bands like Powderfinger and Silverchair pack stadiums around Australia. Singer-songwriter Alex Lloyd's experimental sounds on his 1999 album, *Black the Sun*, and his later singles have won rave reviews.

Pop Princess

Kylie Minogue (1968–) first performed at the age of eleven in a television series called *Skyways*. In 1986, she starred as Charlene, the tomboy mechanic, in the popular soap *Neighbors*. Minogue launched her singing career with "Locomotion" in 1987. She is now an international pop sensation.

LITERATURE

Australia has a literacy rate of nearly 100 percent, and Australians are among the world's biggest book buyers. There are also free public libraries in every town.

Early Books

One of the first Australian classics was the bleak prisoner tale *For the Term of His Natural Life* (1874) by Marcus Clarke. In *Robbery Under Arms* (1889), author Rolf Boldrewood continued the outlaw theme with his story about a tough **bushranger.**

The Golden Years of Literature

In the 1880s, a new understanding of what it meant to be Australian emerged with the help of the literary magazine *The Bulletin*. Its founder, J. F. Archibald, published poems, short stories, and articles about **outback** Australia. One of *The Bulletin's* most famous writers was Henry Lawson (1867–1922). In his story "The Drover's Wife" (1892), he captures the loneliness and courage of a woman on an isolated outback farm.

A. B. "Banjo" Patterson (1864–1941) created well-known characters in his bush ballads *Clancy of the Overflow* (1889) and *The Man from Snowy River* (1890). Patterson's rollicking stories are still widely read. He also wrote "Waltzing Matilda" (1895), Australia's unofficial national anthem.

The autobiographical novel *My Brilliant Career* by Miles Franklin (1879–1954) describes the struggle of a talented woman writer in the early 1900s. Henry Handel Richardson (1870–1946) also took a man's name to get published. Her moving three-volume novel *The Fortunes of Richard Mahony* describes her father's troubled life in early Victoria.

Teen Themes

Paul Jennings *(left)* writes quirky, comical stories for teens. His best-sellers include *Unreal!* and *Uncanny!* Isobelle Carmody writes for older teens. Her *Obernewtyn* fantasies explore serious themes in a magical world. Maureen McCarthy's teen issues novel *Queen Kat, Carmel & St Jude Get a Life* was made into a successful television miniseries.

Modern Writers

Novelist Patrick White (1912–1990) is known for his complex plots and unusual characters. *The Tree of Man* (1955) and *Voss* (1957) are his best-known works. White won the Nobel Prize for Literature in 1973. Other famous writers include the poet Judith Wright (1915–2000) and Christina Stead (1902–1983), who wrote the bitter family saga *The Man Who Loved Children*.

Today's most popular writers include Tim Winton, whose award-winning novels include *Cloudstreet* and *Dirt Music*. In addition, Elizabeth Jolley, whose dark, psychological novels such as *The Well, My Father's Moon* have won many awards. Peter Carey has also received many prizes for his works, from the darkly comic first novel, *Bliss* (1981), to his Booker Prize–winning novels *Oscar and Lucinda* (1988) and *True History of the Kelly Gang* (2000).

Picture Books

May Gibbs (1877–1969) introduced her bush babies to Australian children in 1916 in *Gumnut Babies*. The book includes her charming illustrations of bush flowers, animals, and characters such as the Bad Banksia Men. Renowned artist Norman Lindsay wrote and illustrated the classic *The Magic Pudding* in 1918. Also among Australia's best-loved children's books is *Possum Magic*, written by Mem Fox in 1983 and exquisitely illustrated by Julie Vivas. Jeannie Baker uses shells, plants, feathers, and glue to create collage pictures. Her books on environmental themes include award-winners *Where the Forest Meets the Sea* and *Window*.

The Pudding

THE MAGIC PUDDING

The Magic Pudding, written and illustrated by Norman Lindsay, has remained in print since it was first published in 1918.

FILM
and Television

Australian actors and filmmakers are known worldwide. This is not surprising, as the country was the birthplace of feature films. Actors, directors, and technicians have helped to shape Australia's culture through both film and television.

Film Pioneers

The world's first silent feature film, *The Sign of the Cross*, was made by Major Joseph Perry of the Salvation Army and shown in Melbourne in 1900. Six years later, the Tait brothers put together an hour-long film about the famous bushranger Ned Kelly, titled *The Story of the Kelly Gang*.

Raymond Longford (1878–1959) was the great pioneer of Australian film. As an actor, writer, and director, he produced more than 25 silent films, which are noted for their natural acting style and the places where they were shot. His 1919 love story *The Sentimental Bloke* is now a classic. Longford's partner was the actress, director, and scriptwriter Lottie Lyell (1890–1925). She worked on 20 of Longford's films but died of **tuberculosis** at the age of 35.

The Rebirth of Movies

The Australian film industry declined dramatically when American and British "talkies," or movies with talking and sound, arrived around 1930. Nevertheless, government backing in the 1970s helped bring about a rebirth. *Picnic at Hanging Rock* (1975), directed by Peter Weir, is often named as the greatest Australian film. Weir went on to direct *Dead Poets' Society* (1989), about a gifted English teacher, and the seafaring adventure *Master and Commander* (2003). *My Brilliant Career* (1979), about Australian writer Miles Franklin, was renowned director Gillian Armstrong's first full-length feature film. Her sensitive treatment of characters also shone out in *Little Women* (1994) and *Oscar and Lucinda* (1997). Recent successes include director Baz Luhrmann's modern classics *Romeo and Juliet* (1996) and *Moulin Rouge!* (2001).

The Wiggles

"Wake up, Jeff!" This is a call familiar to millions of toddlers around the world. Murray Cook, Anthony Field, Greg Page, and Jeff Fatt are The Wiggles. Formed in 1991, the group's gentle mix of music, dance, and storytelling has made them a sensation. They have sold more records and videos than Kylie Minogue, and their trademark primary-colored tops can be seen from Taiwan to New York City.

Superstars

Actor Mel Gibson shot to fame when he starred in the action movie *Mad Max* (1979). Oscar-winner Nicole Kidman is recognized as a fine actor in demanding roles, such as her portrayal of Virginia Woolf in *The Hours* (2003). Cate Blanchett provides brilliant character studies in the films *Elizabeth* (1998) and *Charlotte Gray* (2001). Hugh Jackman's talent ranges from singing in stage musicals to playing action heroes in films such as *X-Men* (2000). Eric Bana thrilled audiences in *The Hulk* (2003), while Heath Ledger went from teen idol to serious actor in the film *Ned Kelly* (2003).

Television

Television came to Australia in 1956. There are now three commercial networks, as well as the Australian Broadcasting Commission (ABC), a public broadcaster, and the Special Broadcasting Service (SBS), which caters to Australia's many **ethnic groups.** In addition to American, British, and local sitcoms and dramas, reality series and house and garden makeover shows attract large audiences. And Australian soap operas such as *Neighbors* and *Home and Away* are popular around the world.

Nicole Kidman starred in the film *Moulin Rouge!*, directed by Australian Baz Luhrmann.

The Australian-made soap opera *Neighbors* began in 1985 and is now shown in more than 50 countries.

SPORTS
and Leisure

Australia's open spaces and sunny climate help explain why its people love both sports and the outdoors. Most children are taught swimming and other sports at school. Nevertheless, Australian adults are more likely to watch sports than play it, and almost half the adult population is overweight. Popular leisure activities include camping, going to the beach, boating, hiking, and outdoor dining at cafés or family barbecues.

Champions

Australian athletes excel in international competition. The Australian cricket team is one of the world's best. Wheelchair tennis player David Hall won world championships in 1995, 1998, 2000, 2002, and 2003. He also won a gold medal at the Sydney **Paralympic Games.** Australians invented the Australian crawl swimming stroke, and Olympic champion Ian Thorpe is an international star. Legendary runner Cathy Freeman was the world's fastest woman in the 400 meters when she retired in 2003. Australian golfers and tennis players have won some of the world's major tournaments such as Wimbledon in tennis and the Masters in golf. Yacht racer John Bertrand on *Australia II* stunned the world by winning the America's Cup yacht race in 1983—the first time in 132 years that the United States had not won it.

World champion sprinter Cathy Freeman lit the flame to open the 2000 Sydney Olympics.

The Melbourne Cup is one of the world's great horse races.

Australian Rules Football

Australian rules football began in Melbourne. It developed from rugby and an Aboriginal game called *marngrook*, which featured kicking and high-catching with a possum-skin ball. Tom Wills was the first to write down the rules in 1859. He also founded the Melbourne Football Club, which is the oldest in the world. Australian rules football is now a national passion, with eleven million supporters and half a million players around the country. Grand Final Day each September is a national event, with street parades, big-name stars, and live television coverage.

Cricket

Cricket is extremely popular in Australia. It was invented by the English and arrived with the first prisoners. It involves hitting a small, hard ball with a wooden paddle, then running down a straight course called the pitch. The bowler, or pitcher, aims at three stakes in the ground, called stumps, lined up behind the batter. If the batter hits them, he or she is out. He or she is also out if the ball is caught after it is hit. There are eleven players on each team, and games can last up to five days.

Horse Racing

The Melbourne Cup was first run in 1861 at the Flemington Racecourse. Today, it is one of the world's most famous horse races. Held on the first Tuesday in November, the Melbourne Cup is reason enough for a state holiday, and the rest of Australia stops to listen to the race.

The wonder horse Phar Lap won 37 out of 51 starts from 1929 to 1932. Known for his ability to come from behind to win, he became a symbol of hope for ordinary people during the desperate times of the **Great Depression.** Phar Lap won the Melbourne Cup in 1930. He died suddenly in 1932 in the United States.

ART AND DESIGN

Ancient indigenous artists created Dreamtime stories on cave walls. They also painted their bodies for ceremonies, and elders drew symbolic maps of sacred sites in sand paintings. When Europeans arrived in Australia, they struggled to make sense of its burning light, featureless plains, and ragged trees. The artists among them at first painted gentle, English-looking landscapes. Architects built cramped terrace houses, in spite of the vast open spaces available. It was a century before European art and design truly reflected the land.

Indigenous Art

In 1971, a teacher named Geoffrey Bardon arrived in the remote Papunya community in the Northern Territory, west of Alice Springs. He suggested that the local people paint a mural on the school wall. Bardon recognized their talent and encouraged them to sell their work. So the Western Desert Art Movement began. The first paintings depicted sacred objects, which upset other Aboriginal people. In response, the Papunya artists adopted the now famous dot style to disguise sacred symbols. Today, indigenous artists all over Australia are producing highly prized works.

Desert Dreaming

Clifford Possum Tjapaltjarri (1932–2002) of Central Australia worked as a stockperson before becoming one of Australia's most celebrated indigenous artists. One of the Papunya artists, his spectacular paintings express his Dreaming, or spiritual beliefs, and his desert homeland. Tjapaltjarri was famous in New York City and his home country and was awarded the **Order of Australia** in 2002.

Mulga Seed Dreaming **(1983) was painted by famous indigenous artist Clifford Possum Tjapaltjarri.**

In Lin Onus's 1991 sculpture *Fruit Bats*, 95 fiberglass fruit bats hang upside down from a Hill's Hoist clothesline. They are painted in traditional colored cross-hatching.

Johnny Warangkula Tjupurrula (1925–2001) was also a desert artist pioneer. In the painting *Bushfire Dreaming* (1976), he used his technique of layering patterns to give depth, drawing the viewer into the landscape.

Gloria Petyarre (1946–) is one of the Anmatyerre people in the Northern Territory. She began painting in the late 1980s. She became famous for her energetic, **abstract** works and unusual use of bright colors, including mauves and pinks. Petyarre has won many awards, including one for her painting *Bush Leaves* in 1998.

Emily Kame Kngwarreye (1910–1996) took up art in her 70s in her Central-Australian community of Utopia. She based her paintings on her peoples' dreaming and produced modern, abstract works famous for their fine, energetic use of color. She had her first solo exhibition at the age of 80 in Sydney in 1990 and gained instant success. Her works are in demand around the world.

Albert Namatjira

The most popular artist of his day, Albert Namatjira (1902–1959) was one of the Arrernte people of Central Australia. A highly talented artist, Namatjira painted watercolor landscapes in the European style and was known for his striking use of color. Fame did not save him from racist policies, however. In 1958, he was jailed for selling alcohol to fellow Aborigines. He died the following year.

The Heidelberg School

Around 1887, the young artist Tom Roberts and his friends decided to avoid studios and paint outdoors. For the first time, they captured the harsh Australian light, the blue bush haze, and the dignity of ordinary people. They formed what became known as the Heidelberg School.

Roberts (1856–1931) created one of Australia's most famous paintings, *Shearing the Rams* (1890), which shows a scene in a busy shearing shed. His huge work *Opening of Parliament* (1903) includes more than 250 miniature portraits of official guests at the first session of the Australian Parliament.

Fredrick McCubbin (1855–1917) was a close friend of Roberts. McCubbin is best known for his three-part painting *The Pioneers* (1904), which traces the taming of the bush by a pioneer couple. Arthur Streeton is famous for his light-filled landscapes, such as *Australia Felix* (1907).

Tom Roberts's famous painting *Shearing the Rams* captures the essence of outback Australia.

Garden Design

She was a strong woman in a man's world, but Edna Walling (1895–1973) made gardens of great peace and beauty. As a designer and gardener, she had a huge influence on Australian gardening styles, preferring wild, natural effects; winding stone paths; and simple water features. Later in life, she helped increase the popularity of Australian native plants. Her surviving gardens are national treasures.

Modern Masters

During the 1940s, new, modern styles of painting emerged. Russell Drysdale (1912–1981) arrived in Australia from England at the age of eleven. The deserted towns, lanky figures, and harsh colors in his paintings *Sofala* (1947) and *The Cricketers* (1948) express the toughness of country life.

Sidney Nolan (1917–1992) is best known for his *Ned Kelly* series, begun in 1946. He shows the **bushranger** in his armor as a distinctive black, square-headed figure. Influenced by Aboriginal painting, Nolan's work features strong colors, flat horizons, and **mythical** figures.

John Olsen (1928–) creates **abstract** oils and watercolors that capture the subtle beauty of the Australian landscape and its birds and animals. Olsen's mural *Salute to Five Bells* (1973), a tribute to Kenneth Slessor's famous poem, can be seen in the Sydney Opera House.

Architecture

Australia's two most famous architectural works were both designed by foreigners. Walter Burley Griffin (1876–1937) was an Illinois architect, but his plans for the capital city Canberra were sensitive to the natural landscape and included avenues, waterways, and gardens. He was eventually fired in 1921, but the city's huge lake is named after him.

The Sydney Opera House is one of the world's great buildings. Danish architect Joern Utzon won a competition for the design in 1957. Begun in 1959, the project took fourteen years to complete and cost fourteen times the original estimate. Disputes between Utzon and local officials also led to this architect being fired, as well as to key changes in his design.

Going Forward

Australians regard their culture with confidence. They enjoy exploring bold new ideas, while also being aware of the richness of the past, both **indigenous** and European. The challenge for the future is to weave these two cultural strands together into one many-textured fabric.

GLOSSARY

abstract not realistic or not easy to understand

Anglo-Celtic English-Irish

asylum safe place

bugle brass instrument like a small trumpet

bushranger Australian robber and outlaw

Christianity religion based on the belief in one God and the teachings of Jesus, as written in the Bible. A follower of Christianity is called a Christian.

Commonwealth word used to describe all the states and territories of Australia joined together into one nation

compulsory required by law

constellation group of stars that forms some kind of pattern or shape

corruption dishonesty or criminal behavior for personal gain, especially in reference to government officials or other powerful people

debut to be the very first

democracy form of government in which people make decisions about their government

discriminate to treat people unfairly on the basis of their race, gender, religion, or for some other reason

ecotourism kind of tourism that fosters environmental and cultural conservation and appreciation

egalitarian every person being equal

endangered to be in danger of becoming extinct, or disappearing

ethnic relating to a racial or cultural group

ethnic diversity made up of many different races and cultures

ethnic group group of people who share a specific culture, language, and background

extinct when a species dies out

fertility (rate) average number of children per woman

global warming tendency of the atmosphere to warm up, raising temperatures on Earth

Great Depression period from 1929 to the late 1930s of a worldwide economic downturn, which caused widespread poverty and unemployment

greenhouse gases gases from cars and factories that change the chemistry of the world's atmosphere, making the climate warmer

immigration restrictions rules to prevent foreigners from settling in a country

independence freedom from foreign rule

indigenous original or native person of a particular country or area

inhale to breathe in

land clearance cutting down of natural trees and scrubs for farming

land rights term used to describe what the indigenous peoples of Australia wanted from the government, the rights to the original lands before Europeans arrived

mate term Australians use meaning friend

monarch hereditary leader of a government or country such as a king or queen, often with limited powers

mosque building in which Muslims worship

multicultural made up of several different races and cultures

mythical from fantasy or ancient stories

Order of Australia award for distinguished service to Australia

outback remote area of Australia

Paralympic Games Olympic sports competition for disabled athletes

penal colony prison settlement in a new country ruled by the homeland

reconciliation harmony, friendliness, and peace between people

referendum vote of all the adult population on a particular political issue

regatta yacht race

remedy way of healing the sick

republic country in which people elect representatives to rule for them

sexism attitude that discriminates against people because of their sex

soprano singer who sings the highest part

status level in society

tolerance acceptance of different ways and beliefs

tuberculosis disease of the lungs

INDEX